D1357102

995160833 7

For Aurélien. **K.**

For my little Louison and her love for cats. **M. L.**

It doesn't matter if we're big or small,
we all carry the same emotions in our hearts.
They rest within us, like little seeds, waiting to grow.
This is the story of how sadness grew, one day, in Olive's heart.

Kochka

Quarto is the authority on a wide range of topics.
Quarto educates, entertains and enriches the lives of
our readers—enthusiasts and lovers of hands-on living.
www.quartoknows.com

This edition first published in 2021
by words & pictures,
an imprint of The Quarto Group.
The Old Brewery, 6 Blundell Street,
London N7 9BH, United Kingdom.
T (0)20 7700 6700 F (0)20 7700 8066
www.quartoknows.com

English language edition © 2021 Quarto Publishing plc

Original edition, *Un bol de tristesse pour Nour*,
in French © 2018 Flammarion
Author: Kochka
Illustrator: Marie Leghima

A catalogue record for this book is available from the British Library.

ISBN: 978-0-7112-5863-1

9 8 7 6 5 4 3 2 1
Manufactured in RRD, China
RD112020

WHAT A FEELING!

A Cat with no Name

A STORY ABOUT SADNESS

Written by
KOCHKA

Illustrated by
MARIE LEGHIMA

Notes for parents by
LOUISON NIELMAN

words & pictures

It was breakfast time
in Olive's house.

Olive went downstairs, opened
the fridge and looked inside.

She was hungry!

But just as Olive sat down to eat,
she heard a sound at the window.
A kitten!

She picked up her stool and
went to take a closer look.

Very quietly and carefully,
she opened the window...

... and the kitten jumped inside!

"Hello! Would you like some breakfast?" Olive asked her furry visitor.

The kitten purred as Olive poured some milk into a bowl.

Just then, Olive's mum came into the kitchen.
"Oh!" she gasped. "Who's this?"

"She came through the window," Olive said excitedly.
"Please can we keep her, Mum? Please?"

Mum looked at the neat, clean kitten.
"I think she might already have an owner, Olive.
She must be lost. We can keep her safe here for now,
but when someone comes to find her, she'll have to go home."

Olive was delighted.
"Did you hear that, little kitty?
You can stay here with me!"

Olive loved spending time with the kitten. They played together, walked together, and at bedtime the kitten curled up on Olive's bed.

Whenever the kitten wanted to go outside, Olive opened the window to let her out. At first, Olive worried that she wouldn't return.

But the kitten kept coming back.
And a week later, the kitten was still living with Olive.
"You're my friend now," Olive told her.
"I hope you can stay here forever!"

But on the eighth day, the kitten didn't return.
And she didn't appear the next day, either.

Olive and Dad went out searching for her.
They posted flyers and asked everyone in town
if they'd seen a small, black and white kitten.

When they went into the bakery, they got some news.

"Oh yes," said the baker. "I saw a black and white kitten outside the shop yesterday. Just as I bent down to stroke her, a little girl shouted:

Stella!

and the kitten jumped straight into her arms.

Her mum told me the kitten had run away –
they'd been looking for her for days.
The little girl was so happy to have found her kitten again."

Olive's heart sank. She wanted the kitten to live with her, not the other girl. They'd had such fun together.

"Oh, Olive," said Dad. "I know you loved having Stella around, but she belonged to someone else. She found her way back home again, and that's good, isn't it?"

In the cafe, Olive started to cry. Tears fell into her mug.
"I miss her, Dad," she sobbed.

"I know." Dad said.
"It was so kind of you to take care of her. She chose you
to look after her and I'm sure she'll never forget you."

Olive wiped her eyes. "Are you sure, Dad?" she asked.

"Of course," said Dad.

"And you'll never forget her, either.
The name 'stella' means star, so every night
when you look up into the sky, you'll remember her."

"Yes," Olive said, starting to smile.
"Every night."

NOTES FOR PARENTS, CARERS AND TEACHERS

WHAT IS SADNESS?

It doesn't matter if we're big or small, we all feel sad sometimes.
Sadness rises like a wave and it can last for a few minutes or for days.

Some children will verbilise when they are sad, but others cannot identify when they feel sad, or don't allow themselves to.

Doing badly on a test, being teased, a friend moving away, losing a pet... these are all events that can cause sadness.

Sadness can manifest itself in different ways. A loss of interest in activities, loss of appetite, quietness, and heightened sensitivity are all signs of sadness.

While it might be tempting to minimise sadness by assuring children it will pass, **acknowledging and validating sadness is the best way to help children deal with this emotion.**

If you notice a change in your child's behaviour, you can help them put it into words. Olive's father is the first to identify his daughter's emotional state when they discover that the kitten is back with its owner. It is after he has discussed the situation with her that she starts to cry. Perhaps if Olive's dad hadn't said anything, she would have kept it all in, denied her emotions, and it would have been harder to bear. **It is essential to comfort children.**

WHAT DOES YOUR CHILD NEED FROM YOU?

- For sadness to be recognised and acknowledged.

- To know that they can speak without judgement.

- To feel safe to cry as often as needed.

Sadness should pass with time, but sometimes it doesn't. If your child is struggling to find joy or spontaneity, and their condition worsens, it may be useful to consult a professional.

TIPS FOR WHEN A CHILD IS SAD

- Even if it seems exaggerated to you, try to **avoid downplaying sadness.**

- **Comfort them with things they love or enjoy**, such as their favourite food, hugs, kind words, or a fun activity.

- **Pay them extra attention** for a few days.

- If they can't vocalise their feelings, **encourage them them to draw how they feel**.

- **Help them rate their sadness** between 0 and 5, 1 being a little sad, and 5 being intense sorrow.

- **Touch base with them**; they may be more willing to speak after some time has passed.

Louison Nielman
Clinical Psychologist & Psychotherapist